D0515619

FEARLESS:

TYPICALLY DESCRIBES ONE WHO IS DETERMINED AND COURAGEOUS; WHO OVERCOMES FEAR.

FAIRY TALES OF
Fearless Girls

SUSANNAH McFARLANE

ALADDIN

NEW YORK LONDON TORONTO SYDNEY NEW DELHI

ALADDIN

An imprint of Simon & Schuster Children's Publishing Division

1230 Avenue of the Americas, New York, New York 10020

First Aladdin hardcover edition October 2020

Text copyright © 2018 by Susannah McFarlane

Cover illustrations copyright 2020: Cinderella © Lucinda Gifford; Thumbelina © Sher Rill Ng; Rapunzel © Beth Norling; Little Red Riding Hood and wolf © Claire Robertson; birds © Bipsun/Shutterstock; squirrels © Potapov Alexander/Shutterstock; vines © Natalyon/Shutterstock; grass © NadzeyaShanchuk/Shutterstock.

Illustrations on pages 1-30 & pi copyright © 2018 by Beth Norling

Illustrations on pages 31-58 & pv copyright © 2018 by Claire Robertson

Illustrations on pages 59-88, pvi & p 120 copyright © 2018 by Lucinda Gifford

Illustrations on pages 89-118 & pvii copyright © 2018 by Sher Rill Ng

Originally published in Australia in 2018 by Allen & Unwin as *Fairytales for Feisty Girls*

All rights reserved, including the right of reproduction in whole or in part in any form.

ALADDIN and related logo are registered trademarks of Simon & Schuster, Inc.

For information about special discounts for bulk purchases, please contact Simon & Schuster Special Sales at 1-866-506-1949 or business@simonandschuster.com.

The Simon & Schuster Speakers Bureau can bring authors to your live event. For more information or to book an event contact the Simon & Schuster Speakers Bureau at 1-866-248-3049 or visit our website at www.simonspeakers.com.

Jacket designed by Sandra Nobes and Karin Paprocki

Interior designed by Sandra Nobes

The text of this book was set in Horley Old Style.

Manufactured in the United States of America 0720 FFG

2 4 6 8 10 9 7 5 3 1

Library of Congress Cataloging-in-Publication Data

Names: McFarlane, Susannah, author. | Norling, Beth, illustrator. | Robertson, Claire, 1972- illustrator. | Gifford, Lucinda, illustrator. | Ng, Sher Rill, illustrator.

Title: Fairy tales of fearless girls / Susannah McFarlane ; Beth Norling, Lucinda Gifford, Claire Robertson, Sher Rill Ng.

Description: First Aladdin hardcover edition. | New York : Aladdin, 2020. | Originally published: Crows Nest, Australia : Allen & Unwin, 2018. | Audience: Ages 5-9. | Summary: Reimagines four classic fairy tales with a feminist twist.

Identifiers: LCCN 2020019072 (print) | LCCN 2020019073 (ebook) | ISBN 9781534473577 (hardback) | ISBN 9781534473584 (ebook)

Subjects: CYAC: Fairy tales. | Conduct of life—Fiction. | Feminism—Fiction.

Classification: LCC PZ8 .M45787 Fai 2020 (print) | LCC PZ8 .M45787 (ebook) | DDC [Fic]—dc23

LC record available at https://lccn.loc.gov/2020019072

CONTENTS

For Robin
With love and gratitude for
real-life happily ever afters

ONCE UPON A TIME, *in a land far away*
(yet not so different from today),
four young girls stand and fight
for what is good; for what is right.

Dark forces try to hold them back.
Evil tempts them from the track.
In order to be truly free,
these girls must strong and fearless be.

In the darkness they find the light,
cleverness triumphing over might.
And when others do them wrong,
in their softness they are strong.

They may be small, but they're big of heart—
kind and cheerful, brave and smart.
And so with courage, hope and laughter
they make their own "happily ever after."

Rapunzel

1.

ONCE upon a time, in a village on the edge of a forest, there lived a woman and her husband. Their village was overshadowed by a dark stone castle belonging to an enchantress.

The enchantress was old, and regaining her youth was the one thing her magic powers could not conjure. This made the enchantress bitter, and the more the bitterness grew in her heart, the meaner she became.

So the enchantress conjured up around her what she could not achieve in herself, and the castle garden teemed with sweet, magical flowers of every kind and color. The flowers were never cut, and they never faded, blooming within the high castle wall all year round. Yet as the castle was charmed, the surrounding village was cursed: its gardens died; the crops in the fields failed; and no babies were born. The villagers lost hope, and now bitterness also cloaked the village.

One day, with great joy and surprise, the woman and her husband discovered that they were to have a child. Yet their joy was short-lived, for as the child grew inside her, the woman became sick: her belly pained her, and a bitter taste formed in her mouth that not even the sweetest honey could remove. As her belly swelled, so too did this strange illness.

Lying on her bed one afternoon, the woman looked out of the window to see a lush green rapunzel plant growing through a crack in the castle wall, its bright-blue flowers glowing in the sunlight. The woman began to crave the plant's bitter leaves, and soon she could think of nothing else but how much she wanted to eat the rapunzel, believing that it, and it alone, would cure her illness.

The husband fetched the plant for his wife, and as she devoured the bitter leaves, the taste in her mouth sweetened and the pain in her belly eased. For the first time in weeks, she slept soundly that night, but by morning the pain had returned.

The woman asked her husband to fetch more rapunzel, but there was no more of the plant growing outside the castle wall, and the husband was afraid to enter the garden of the enchantress. Yet as his wife's groans grew louder and he thought she would surely die, he could bear it no longer. So that night, and every night following, he scaled the castle wall and jumped into the garden to steal more rapunzel.

One moonlit night, the enchantress discovered the husband in her garden.

"You! Thief!" she hissed.

"How dare you enter my garden and steal my rapunzel!"
And she raised her hands to cast a terrible spell upon him.

"Please, I beg you, let me take it to save my wife and unborn child," pleaded the husband.

A child! Youth! The enchantress smiled a terrible, scheming smile.

"I will release you," she said, "and you may take all the rapunzel you can carry— but on one condition."

"Thank you, thank you!" exclaimed the husband. "Anything!"

"You will give me your child on the very day it is born."

Horrified, the husband refused at first, but he loved his wife

and, believing that she and the baby would die without the rapunzel, in the end he agreed.

And so it was. The baby, a girl, was born, and the enchantress appeared at the door of the cottage to claim her. She took the baby and carried her away to raise her as her own, behind the castle wall. The woman and her husband moved far, far away, and no one in the village ever saw the girl again, although it was rumored that the enchantress had named her Rapunzel, after the bitter-leafed plant for which she was the payment.

2.

THE BABY GREW into a sweet girl, with eyes as blue as rapunzel flowers and glowing, golden locks. The rapunzel plant her mother had eaten had enchanted her hair: it grew never-endingly long, strong and thick, and it gleamed like nothing else the enchantress had ever seen.

"So beautiful," she would croon as she stroked and braided Rapunzel's hair. "I am your mother, and you, child, are mine—mine alone and mine always."

Rapunzel often wouldn't reply at first, for she was always busy doing something else—folding pieces of parchment into creatures, or stacking her trinket chests to build tall towers.

"Rapunzel?" the enchantress would repeat.

"Sorry, Mother," Rapunzel would reply absentmindedly. "Look what I've made!"

But the enchantress was never interested in Rapunzel's creations, and Rapunzel would sigh. Sometimes she thought the only thing the enchantress cared about was her hair.

Indeed, the enchantress did love all things beautiful. Fearing that Rapunzel might be stolen from her just like her rapunzel plant, one day she took the girl from the castle and locked her in a tall tower in the middle of the forest.

The tower had only one room with one window, right at the very top, and there were neither doors nor stairs.

Red climbing roses twined around the tower. They flooded the room with their fragrance, but entangled the tower's walls like barbed wire with their sharp, cruel thorns. The only way into the room was to climb up on Rapunzel's hair, which the enchantress did every day.

"Rapunzel, Rapunzel, let down your golden hair!" she would cry from the bottom of the tower.

"Look out below!" Rapunzel would shout back.

Rapunzel would unwind her braid, sling it around a hook above the window, and let it tumble to the ground. Then the enchantress would climb up the braid and through the window.

Rapunzel was happy in her tower. Unlike the rapunzel plant, she did not have a hint of bitterness in her; she always saw the best in everything. The enchantress had filled the tower room with many beautiful things: gold-framed mirrors, in front of which she would brush Rapunzel's hair; bejeweled dresses of silk and taffeta; fine necklaces and bracelets in a small, exquisitely crafted glass chest; a lute; luxurious cushions to lie on. Rapunzel saw these items' beauty, but she also saw something else . . . building materials. For Rapunzel had a very special gift indeed, the gift of imagination and invention.

One day, for example, when Rapunzel's enormous braid was feeling even heavier to her than usual, she looked at the ornately carved wooden chest in the corner of her room.

Rapunzel thought. Rapunzel sketched. Rapunzel planned and pondered. Then Rapunzel built.

Using bed knobs for wheels and a long pearl necklace for rope, she converted the chest into a cart, so that she could pull her heavy braid along behind her. Now, with a new lightness of head, Rapunzel could think more clearly and move more freely. Hands on hips, cart behind her, she looked around the room again. She spied the curtain rings above the window, and it wasn't long before Rapunzel had made herself a game of quoits to play.

When the enchantress arrived later that day, she was dismayed. "What have you done, Rapunzel?" she cried. "Your beautiful chest! Your pearls!"

"Yes, Mother," replied Rapunzel cheerily. "Now they are beautiful *and* they move! Would you like to play quoits?"

The enchantress did not want to play quoits. She only wanted Rapunzel to be still, so that she could brush her long, heavy hair.

Rapunzel had other ideas, though. Another day, she eyed her four-poster bed.

Rapunzel thought. Rapunzel sketched. Rapunzel planned and pondered.

Then Rapunzel built, and soon after, the four-poster bed became a two-poster as Rapunzel built herself some stilts.

The enchantress did not approve of the stilts. "Rapunzel," she exclaimed, "get down from there—it's not safe!"

"But they're brilliant, Mother," cried Rapunzel. "I can touch the roof!"

And so time went on in the tower. Rapunzel built a step to make it easier for the enchantress when she came through the window; that was one invention the enchantress did approve of.

She built a bed-making system out of curtain sashes. And, with the shutters from the window, she invented a candle-powered fan for the hot summer months ahead of her.

Rapunzel was always building something new in her tower.

3.

ONE SUMMER'S DAY, something a little different happened. Up high on her stilts, Rapunzel discovered a small hole in the tower roof, and that gave her a new idea.

Rapunzel thought. Rapunzel sketched. Rapunzel planned and pondered. Then Rapunzel built.

She enlarged the hole and, with some glass from her jewelry chest, crafted a window. She stood on her stilts looking up at the fluffy white clouds rolling by.

The enchantress was not pleased. "Rapunzel," she exclaimed, "what have you done?"

"But, Mother," Rapunzel protested, "it's brilliant!"

The next day, the enchantress brought a length of heavy, scarlet velvet to cover the new window.

"Oh, thank you, Mother," said Rapunzel, eyeing the strength of the fabric.

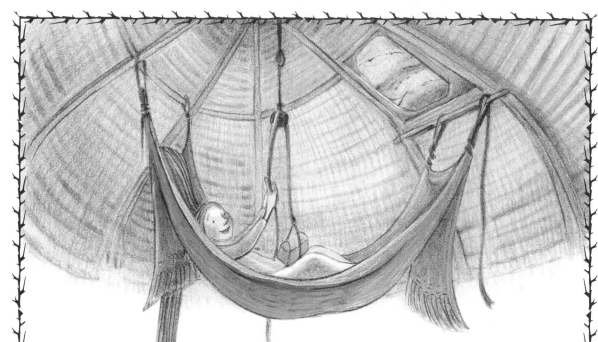

When the enchantress had left, Rapunzel lost no time converting the fabric into a sturdy hammock slung between two rafters next to the window. Then, throwing a hair ribbon over one rafter and attaching it to her jewelry box, Rapunzel also made a pulley, so that she could raise snacks up to herself as she lay in her sky-gazing hammock.

"Perfect!" she exclaimed, proud of her work. "Now I can lie and watch the clouds float by in the day and see the stars come out at night—while I eat!"

That night, Rapunzel lay in her hammock, munching on an apple as she gazed up at the night sky. As she did so, she began to wonder what else besides her tower the stars might be twinkling down upon. . . .

The next day, Rapunzel found that she could not stop imagining what lay below her tower, on the side without a window. Seeing her reflection in the large ornate mirror behind her, Rapunzel had another idea.

Rapunzel thought. Rapunzel sketched. Rapunzel planned and pondered. Then Rapunzel built.

She removed the glass from a small vanity mirror and, using a diamond from her necklace, cut it into two. She then took a hollow curtain rod and positioned the glass at a certain angle at each end. Rapunzel had made a periscope, and by standing on her stilts and holding it high so it poked out of her new window, she could now see what was on the other side: a glorious waterfall, with torrents of water glittering in the sunlight and crashing down onto the rocks below.

"How *amazing*!" exclaimed Rapunzel. "I wonder what else is to be seen outside this tower."

"Mother," she said as she had her hair brushed and braided later that day, "what is the world like? May I see it?"

The enchantress paused in her braiding. "Oh, no," she replied, winding the heavy braid tightly around the girl's head, pulling at Rapunzel's hair just a little too hard. "The world outside is full of thieves, and here, in this tower, you are safe. You must never leave it."

But Rapunzel wasn't sure she wanted to be safe. She was beginning to think she wanted to see the world instead—or at least more of it than she could see from her windows.

She did not want to upset the enchantress, though, so she simply smiled and answered, "Of course, Mother."

The next day, the enchantress arrived at the tower carrying a yellow canary in an exquisite cage.

"Rapunzel, Rapunzel, let down your golden hair!" she cried. And then, once she had climbed inside: "Here, Rapunzel, isn't it beautiful? It will sing to you."

"Uh . . . thank you, Mother," said Rapunzel—but she found she couldn't smile, for the bird wasn't singing, and its beautiful feathers were already losing their luster.

Rapunzel couldn't bear to see the bird unhappy, so as soon as the enchantress was gone she took the bird from its cage and, stretching her arms out the window, opened her hands. She smiled at last as the bird spread its wings, soared upward and then swooped down the tower and into the forest below.

How Rapunzel longed to follow the bird out of the tower—but she knew now that the enchantress would never take her. Perhaps she could just leave on her own, but how? Was there a way for Rapunzel to get herself down the tower? Rapunzel pondered.

4.

A WEEK OR two later, as Rapunzel was leaning out of her window with her periscope, she saw something emerging from the forest below. She leaned as far as she dared out the new window to get a closer look.

Now she could see a young man on a white horse, riding toward the waterfall. Rapunzel tilted her periscope to see what he did and watched, fascinated, as the man got off his horse, knelt down by the waterfall, took out a scroll, and started to write.

Rapunzel wondered what the man was writing. As she was wondering that, he got back on his horse and rode away. Rapunzel saw that he could come and go as he pleased— that, like the canary, he was free.

Then and there, Rapunzel decided that she would be free too.

She didn't want to disobey or hurt the enchantress, but she knew in her heart that it was time: time to leave the tower, not just for one day to look for building materials, but to start building her life.

The only way for the enchantress to climb up or down the tower was on Rapunzel's hair, but perhaps there was another way.

Rapunzel thought. Rapunzel sketched. Rapunzel planned and pondered.

Could she just climb down the rose branches? She looked out and down the tower wall and saw the jagged thorns. *Ouch,* thought Rapunzel, *that would hurt. Back to the drawing wall.*

A catapult? she thought. She could launch herself out of the window into the forest. She sketched some more. *Too risky,* she decided. After all, where might she land?

Next, Rapunzel thought perhaps she could make a rope from all her dresses. She took them from her wardrobe and measured them, calculating how long her dress-rope would be if she cut them all into strips and joined them up. She frowned as she realized that, however cleverly she cut, her dress-rope would only reach halfway down the tower. *Hmmm,* thought Rapunzel, *and then it would be the thorns again. Back to the drawing wall.*

Rapunzel kept coming back to the thought that the only way up and down was by climbing her hair. When she lowered it for the enchantress, she wound it around the window hook, so that the hook took the weight of the climber. That wouldn't work if Rapunzel *was* the climber.

The enchantress could climb up the hair because she wasn't attached to it. *Therefore,* Rapunzel logically realized, if *she* wasn't attached to it . . . If she cut off her own braid . . .

Excitement and fear struck Rapunzel. The enchantress had told her that she could never leave the tower. And now Rapunzel realized that she was going to do just that.

"And, actually," she said out loud, "I've never liked my long hair—not even a little! It's Mother who loves it."

Rapunzel thought. Rapunzel sketched. Rapunzel planned and pondered.

"And so she can have it," she declared, taking out her cutting diamond. "Rapunzel, Rapunzel, it's time to let go of your hair!"

In one stroke, Rapunzel slashed at her locks. She left some length, so her hair now fell to her shoulders. She looked in a mirror and smiled. She felt light, as if a great weight had been lifted off her shoulders, which of course it had been.

Now all she had to do was tie her braid to the hook and climb down it. She tied her old hair fast, and she was just about to hurl it down the tower wall when the young man on the white horse rode out from the forest again.

And just like that, Rapunzel, remembering
the way the canary had swooped down
the tower, had a better idea.
"Hello, sir!" Rapunzel called out. The young man
looked up. "Will you help me? I need someone
to tie this hair halfway up that big tree."
She pointed to a pine tree
some distance from the tower.
"Fascinating!" called back the
young man. "May I ask why?"
"So I can slide down it."
"Brilliant!" he replied. "Will it reach?"
Good question, Rapunzel thought. She liked
the way this young man thought. "Yes,"
she replied. "I have calculated that if
the braid is tied exactly two lengths
from the ground, it will reach."

So the young man tied the
braid to the tree, according to
her instructions.

"Tied fast?" she called.

"Tied fast!" he replied.

Rapunzel took her lute and broke
off its neck. She put it over
the top of the hair-rope, gripped it hard,
and pulled on it, checking it could
hold her weight.

And then . . . Rapunzel pushed off
from the window.

She flew down her hair,
swooping just like the canary had.
She had never felt so free. As she
approached the tree, Rapunzel
jumped off, landing in a dark-green
bush dotted with small blue flowers.

5.

"THAT WAS AMAZING!" shouted the young man,
running toward Rapunzel.

Rapunzel turned to him. He was about the same age as she
was, and he had kind eyes and a soft face.

"Thank you," she said. "And thank you for your help."

"I *love* how you flew down that tower," said the young man.
"And I like your hair. It's so golden—and such a perfect length."

Rapunzel blushed. "I like your hair too," she said. And it
was true—she did.

"I've also been thinking of building something," said the
man. "A water wheel, to pump water to all the fields around
my castle."

"That's why you came to the waterfall?" asked Rapunzel.

"Yes," said the man. "I was studying its power. I do love to ponder and plan. Would you like to see my village?"

"Yes," said Rapunzel, "very much. But first I need to do something."

She untied her braid from the tree and it sprang back, hanging down from the tower. Then she returned to where she had landed—the dark-green bush—and picked a large bouquet of the lovely blue flowers growing on it. She left them at the bottom of the tower, thinking the enchantress might like them. Rapunzel didn't want her to be sad.

And then Rapunzel and the young man rode away from the tower toward the castle on his white horse. Together, they would build many wonderful things.

The next morning when the enchantress came to the tower, she saw Rapunzel's hair already hanging out the window. Alarmed, she scrambled up the tower and discovered that Rapunzel was gone. Screaming in anger, she climbed back down the tower, and it was then that she saw the flowers. She recognized them immediately. They were from a rapunzel plant.

"Noooooo!" cried the enchantress. "It is over!"

For, without knowing it, in her sweet act of leaving the enchantress the flowers, Rapunzel had repaid the debt of her parents and broken the enchantress's bitter curse.

Rapunzel was free: she no longer belonged to anybody but herself. There was nothing the enchantress could do.

Back at the enchantress's village, the dark stone walls of the castle slowly crumbled, and the villagers' gardens teemed with life once more.

And everyone lived happily ever after.

Little Red Riding Hood

1.

ONCE upon a time, in a small thatched house on the edge of some large woods, lived a girl named Lucy. Most people called her Little Red Riding Hood, though Lucy didn't know why. She was quite tall, and never rode a horse, and while she did have a favorite red cape with a hood, it wasn't the only thing she wore. Yet the name had stuck.

Lucy's grandmother had made the red cape for her by hand and Lucy loved it, especially because Grandma had added special pockets around the cape for her to put her collection jars in. Lucy did a lot of collecting. She collected pine cones, seedpods, and bird feathers, but most of all she collected wildflowers.

Each time Lucy walked the long, winding path leading through the woods to Grandma's house on the other side,

she looked for flowers. She had a sharp eye and she would stop often, inspecting all she saw and using her special scissors to collect flower samples.

Lucy collected flowers she knew her grandmother would use in the potions and lotions she made. Her grandmother knew a special plant cure for almost everything, and Lucy loved to watch her make her treatments using the large mortar and pestle she kept on her kitchen shelf.

Lucy also loved to collect flowers for her botanical journal and was always thrilled when she came across one she'd never seen before. Cutting carefully, she would remove a single flower from the plant and place it in one of her glass collection jars to take home with her.

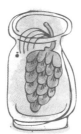

Once home, Lucy would place the new flower into her wooden press, also a gift from Grandma. When the flower was pressed, Lucy would stick it down in her nature journal, and write down both its common name and its Latin name. She found the Latin names in her precious book, *A Botanical Encyclopedia of Woodland Flowers*.

Lucy was very precise with her spelling, and she also noted down important details about each flower, particularly anything Grandma had taught her about its medicinal properties.

Lucy had been collecting wildflowers for a long time, and her journal was nice and fat.

There was, however, one very rare flower that Lucy really, really wanted to find, and she would spend hours stopping on the path in the woods each week searching for it. It was called the drooping tulip, or *Fritillaria meleagris*, a checkered, lily-like bellflower with petals that, as its name suggests, drooped downward.

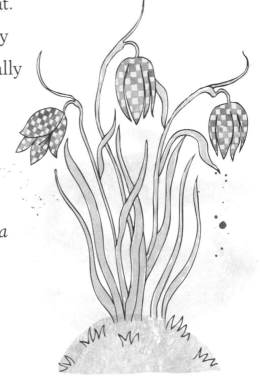

Drooping tulips had been very common when her grandmother was a girl, and Grandma often told Lucy about how they looked like glorious stained glass when the light shone through their checkered petals. Lucy longed to find one and kept her eyes peeled every time she walked in the woods.

2.

ONE DEWY SUMMER morning, Lucy's mother woke her early.

"Please go and visit your grandmother, Lucy," said her mother. "She hasn't been feeling well, so I've made her a nourishing poppy-seed cake, as well as some elderflower cordial, which will do wonders for her cold."

"Poor Grandma!" said Lucy, jumping out of bed. "I'll leave straightaway."

"Good girl," replied her mother, watching with a smile as Lucy pulled on her dress, stockings, boots, and of course, her cape. "But remember, no wandering off the path for wildflowers. The woods can be dangerous!"

"Don't worry, Mother, I won't," cried Lucy, basket in hand and flower jars in pockets, as she skipped out through the back gate leading to the woods, swinging it shut behind her.

Lucy was not the only one walking the woods that morning. Far from the path, a hungry wolf was also out early, prowling around looking for his breakfast. He stopped, lifted his long snout to the breeze, and sniffed.

"Hmmmm," he said, licking his lips. "Something tasty is coming." And he sauntered toward the path.

Meanwhile, Lucy had skipped along the woodland path, around the first turn, until she reached the tall oak tree that marked the beginning of the bluebell grove. Hundreds of beautiful flowers grew along either side of the path here. She stopped to gather a big bunch of them, some for her and some for Grandma.

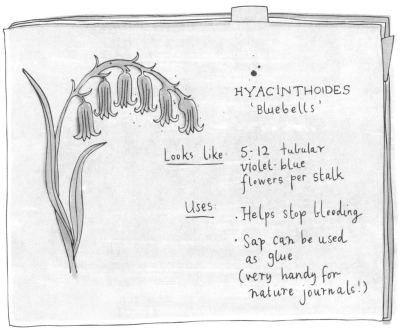

HYACINTHOIDES
'Bluebells'

Looks like: 5-12 tubular violet-blue flowers per stalk

Uses: · Helps stop bleeding

· Sap can be used as glue (very handy for nature journals!)

Lucy continued on her way, and soon enough she came
around the second bend in the path and saw the wolf up ahead.

"Hello, little girl," called the wolf.

"Oh, good morning, Mr. Wolf,"
Lucy replied politely
as she drew closer.
"My name is Lucy."

Now, Lucy had never seen a wolf up close before. Being such a keen observer of nature—fauna as well as flora—she was, of course, keen to study him.

She noted his ears. They were quite small, rather pointy, and dark gray in color, with flecks of white.

She noted his squinty eyes. They were of medium size, and Lucy thought she could detect a glint in them.

And she noted his very big and sharp-looking teeth. Which would be very good for chomping into things, Lucy thought.

The wolf was also interested in Lucy. "What do you have there in your basket, Lucy?" he asked.

"Some poppy-seed cake and elderflower cordial," replied Lucy.

"Delicious!" said the wolf, licking his lips. And while he did think the cake and the cordial sounded very nice indeed, he was thinking more about what a tasty sandwich-filling Lucy would make.

"Where are you off to this fine morning?" continued the wolf, moving a little bit closer.

"I'm going to visit my grandmother. She lives in the house at the end of the path, on the other side of the woods," replied Lucy. "She's not feeling very well, and elderflower cordial is excellent for clearing the head."

Aha! thought the wolf. *I can make a club sandwich with both this little girl and her grandmother. But how will I get to the grandmother before this girl does?*

Then the wolf spied the girl's flower jars, and that gave him an idea.

"You're a flower collector, I see," he said. "Do you know, I passed the most beautiful flower I've ever seen, just beyond the path." And, with his long, furry paw, he gestured vaguely into the woods.

"You did?" said Lucy. "Did it . . . did it look like a bell, by any chance? Did it have a checkered pattern to its petals?"

Of course, the wolf had seen no such flower, but he could tell from the eager look on Lucy's face that it meant a great deal to her, and so he said, "Why yes, it looked exactly like that. It was extremely beautiful and there was just the one."

Lucy could hardly breathe, she was so excited. A drooping tulip, at last! "My goodness!" she said. "They are very rare." She just had to see it; to have it in her collection.

"Are they indeed? Well, it's just through there," replied the wolf, again pointing toward the dark woods.

Lucy knew that she shouldn't leave the path. Her mother had told her not to. But perhaps, just this once . . . for just this one flower?

"Is it far off the path?" she asked the wolf.

"No, no, not at all. It's straight through there," said the wolf, again licking his lips.

Lucy took a deep breath. "Well, thank you, Mr. Wolf," she said. "Thank you very much indeed. You have a nice morning!" And she stepped off the path.

"Oh, I most certainly will, a delightful morning, I expect," replied the wolf, and he turned and ran, full wolf-speed, down the path toward Lucy's grandmother's house.

3.

WHEN THE WOLF reached Lucy's grandmother's house, a little out of breath, he knocked on the door.

"Who is it?" called a raspy voice from inside the cottage.

"It's me, Lucy," cried the wolf, trying to make his voice very high and, he hoped, very little-girl-like.

"Oh, how lovely. Do come in, dear," called Grandma. "Lift the latch. You're just in time for a cup of tea—I've boiled the kettle."

The wolf lifted the latch and walked into the cottage. Grandma turned toward him with a wide smile that soon disappeared from her face. "But you're not—"

She didn't have time to finish her sentence, because the wolf grabbed her, bound her hands with her dressing-gown cord, pushed a silk scarf into her mouth, and shoved her into the large wooden linen chest in the corner of her bedroom.

"Wait there," he growled, pushing her down roughly on top of her nicely folded pillowcases, which smelled of lavender. "I'll be back when I get the other half of my sandwich."

Just before the wolf slammed down the lid of the chest and locked it with the key, Grandma let a bit of her nightgown hang out of the side of the chest. The wolf didn't notice. He was much too busy putting another of Grandma's nightgowns on, as well as a matching nightcap, and climbing into her bed.

"Now to wait," said the wolf, licking his lips with his long, red tongue.

4.

LUCY HAD LOOKED and looked for the drooping tulip, but she couldn't find it anywhere.

Was that wolf imagining things? she wondered, sighing in disappointment.

Just then, she caught a glimpse of brilliant yellow through the undergrowth. "Oh, buttercups!" she exclaimed. "Grandma will be pleased. This is something, at least."

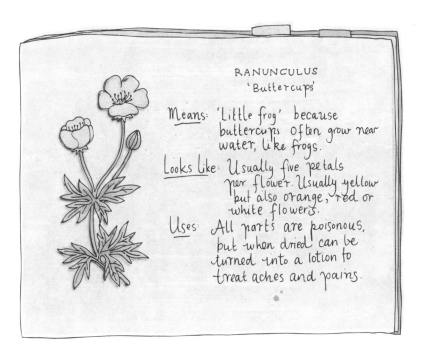

RANUNCULUS
'Buttercups'

Means: 'Little frog' because buttercups often grow near water, like frogs.

Looks Like: Usually five petals per flower. Usually yellow but also orange, red or white flowers.

Uses: All parts are poisonous, but when dried can be turned into a lotion to treat aches and pains.

After gathering a bunch of buttercups, Lucy decided it was high time she returned to the path and her journey.

Lucy was feeling impatient to reach Grandma's now, so she decided to run the rest of the way. Her flower jars jangled as she went.

Just before the third bend in the path, she passed a woodsman. He looked up as she ran by, but Lucy did not want any further distractions, so she kept on running.

A little farther along the path she noticed an axe left in a tree trunk, but she didn't stop to think about that, either.

She kept running, *almost* all the way to her grandmother's house. Just before the path and the woods ended, Lucy caught a flash of red and white on her left and skidded to a halt. Poppies! Since Grandma only ever used a few of these at a time, Lucy used her scissors to carefully cut just three flowers from their stalks. Then she continued on her way.

PAPAVER RHOEAS
'Poppies'

Looks like: Can grow up to one meter high. Stem and leaves covered with coarse hairs.

Uses: A poppy tea helps bring on sleep- but Grandma says you must only ever use half a single teaspoon of the petals or else!

WARNING: Can be TOXIC (Leaves, stems, unripe seeds, some varieties of petals. BEWARE!)

When Lucy arrived at the front gate, she immediately noticed that the front door was open.

That's unusual, thought Lucy as she walked into the cottage.

Next, Lucy noticed steam coming from the kettle, but saw that Grandma's yellow teapot and tea canister were still sitting on the table.

Grandma never leaves her canister out, thought Lucy. She was a little worried now.

"Grandma?" she called out. "Where are you?"

"In here, dear," cried the wolf from the bedroom. Lucy didn't think the voice sounded like Grandma's, but after all, she did have a heavy cold.

However, when Lucy walked into the bedroom, she didn't think whoever was in the bed *looked* like Grandma, either. She bravely moved in for a closer look.

"What pointy ears you have, Grandma!" cried Lucy, as she saw the wolf's furry ears sticking out from the nightcap.

"All the better to hear you with," replied the wolf. "Come closer, my dear." But Lucy wasn't so sure that was a good idea.

"And what squinty eyes you have, Grandma!" she said instead. They now had a most definite glint to them.

"All the better to see you with," replied the wolf.

Of course, Lucy had realized by now that it was the wolf from the woods who was sitting in Grandma's bed, wearing Grandma's nightgown and nightcap. She had also noticed the wolf's particularly big and sharp-looking teeth—but she was definitely not going to comment on those.

Where is Grandma? Lucy wondered. Her eyes darted around the bedroom. Then she caught sight of the small bit of flannel, white with purple lilac (Lucy had given it to her last birthday), sticking out of the side of the linen chest. *Grandma would never put her nightgown in with her linens!* thought Lucy.

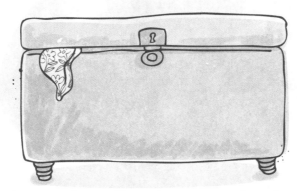

Now she knew where Grandma was—but how could Lucy rescue her? Lucy's heart was beating fast, but her mind was working faster. She looked at the wolf in the bed, she looked down at her flower jars and saw the three poppies, and she remembered the teapot in the kitchen. And then Lucy knew exactly how to help Grandma.

She took a deep breath and looked the wolf straight in the eyes. "Grandma, I'm going to make you your favorite tea!" said Lucy.

"Oh no, dear," said the wolf, a little too quickly and a little harshly. "You don't need to do that. Come here and give me a hug instead."

"Oh yes, Grandma, it would be my pleasure. I know how you love your tea," replied Lucy, turning and walking boldly into the kitchen. "And look, the kettle has already boiled."

Lucy worked quickly. She ground up the red poppies with the mortar and pestle, just like she'd seen Grandma do many times before. Then she added boiling water. Lucy waited a few minutes before pouring the tea into Grandma's favorite fine-china teacup, which was white with red roses.

Lucy carefully carried the teacup into the bedroom and handed it to the wolf.

"Here you are, Grandma," she said. "Your favorite tea."

The wolf still felt a little annoyed, but he did actually quite like tea, so he played along and took a big gulp.

It was only a few seconds before his eyes started to droop. Then the wolf opened his mouth in an enormous yawn.

It's working! thought Lucy. *And, goodness, what big teeth you have. All the better to eat me with, I'll bet. But not today, Mr. Wolf.*

"One more sip of your tea, Grandma," said Lucy to the now very drowsy wolf. "You know you always love the last little bit."

"I do?" mumbled the wolf, his head falling back onto the satin pillow.

"And now," said Lucy, smiling, "what a nice big sleep you are going to have."

And, indeed, the wolf was fast asleep. Lucy ran over to the chest, unlocked it, and opened the lid. She untied her grandmother's hands, took the scarf from her mouth, and helped her out of the chest.

"Grandma, I made your sleepy tea!" she said proudly. "Only stronger . . . *much* stronger."

"Oh, good girl, Lucy!" said her grandmother. "What a clever idea to use *Papaver rhoeas*! And now I think that wolf needs one more thing. Lucy, did you happen to collect any buttercups today?"

"Why yes, I did," replied Lucy, taking the flowers from one of her pockets and handing them to her grandmother.

"Very good," said Grandma. She went to the kitchen and pulled down some jars from the kitchen shelf. "Now, we will

just add a few more things to make
a rather special blend. Lucy, mortar
and pestle at the ready, please!"

Lucy pounded the buttercups, and
Grandma added some more seeds
and then more powders from her jars.
Soon there was a green paste at the
bottom of the mortar.

"Well done!" said Grandma,
smiling proudly at Lucy as she
carried the mortar into the bedroom.

"Now, you greedy wolf, we need to do something about those
teeth," she said as she rubbed the paste onto the sleeping wolf's
gums.

Lucy and Grandma then dragged the wolf outside and onto
a handcart, which, together, they pulled off the path and far
into the woods. As Lucy helped to tip the wolf onto the mossy
ground, she saw that quite a few of his teeth were lying on the
cart's floor.

"No more chomping on little girls or old grandmothers for
this one," said Grandma sternly. "But I'm a little peckish
myself. Let's go and have some morning tea, Lucy."

And so there they left the wolf. They pulled the cart
back to Grandma's cottage, where they sat down to two
slices of poppy-seed cake and two big glasses of elderflower
cordial.

Lucy showed Grandma the other flowers she had collected,
and the latest pages she had recorded in her nature journal.

"Oh, and I have pressed something
special for you, Lucy," said her
grandmother, taking a
red bell-shaped flower from
inside a small box.

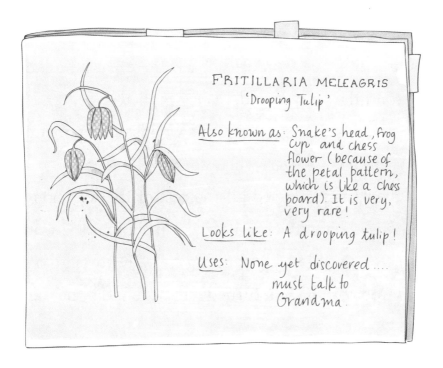

FRITILLARIA MELEAGRIS
'Drooping Tulip'

Also known as: Snake's head, frog cup and chess flower (because of the petal pattern, which is like a chess board). It is very, very rare!

Looks like: A drooping tulip!

Uses: None yet discovered.... must talk to Grandma.

"A drooping tulip!" cried Lucy in delight.

"I rather thought you'd like it," said Grandma, smiling. "Now, my girl, no stopping on the way home, and no—"

"No wandering off the path!" said Lucy.

"Exactly," said Grandma.

And Lucy did stick to the path. On her way home, she passed the woodsman again. He seemed to be searching for something.

"Excuse me," called out Lucy, "you're not looking for an axe, are you?"

"Why, yes!" said the woodsman, looking up. "How did you know? Have you seen it?"

"Yes, it's in a tree trunk just back there past the large oak tree, beyond the path's bend," Lucy replied.

"Oh, yes, of course!" said the woodsman, remembering. "I have been looking everywhere for it. Thank you!"

And then Lucy skipped all the rest of the way home, and everyone lived happily ever after . . . including the wolf, who was last seen toothlessly gumming his way through a pile of soft mushrooms, which, it turned out, he found rather delicious.

Cinderella

1.

ONCE upon a time there was a girl called Ella, who lived with her parents on a rambling, animal-filled manor farm in the countryside of a large kingdom.

Every morning, Ella would wake to the sound of the sparrows chirping in the trees and the ducks quacking in the pond. It was her favorite time of the day and she would rush outside to feed the farm animals, who, as she had no brothers or sisters, were her main companions.

Tess, the old black-and-white sheepdog, would follow Ella faithfully as she scattered seed to the hens (Harriet, Hope, Henrietta, Hattie, and Hilda) and the gamboling geese (Gabriel and Grace). Next, Ella would hurl scraps to the pigs (Peggy and Paul) and round up the many black-spotted dairy cows for milking.

Ella didn't mind the hard and dirty farmwork of cleaning out the pens, hauling sacks of grain, or wading into the pigsty's mud. She was happiest in her rubber boots, amidst the barking and cackling, braying and crowing of her animal friends.

"Morning, everyone!" she would shout, joyfully jumping into every puddle she saw, Tess right behind her.

Once Ella's morning chores were complete, she and her mother would walk in the nearby woods, often returning with an injured bird, a lost lamb, or a rabbit that had been caught in a trap. Ella's mother taught Ella to care for them all with kindness and patience, until they'd healed and could return to the wild.

One chilly winter's day, though, Ella's
mother became ill. Suddenly, there were
no more walks in the woods. Instead of
looking after lost animals, now Ella
looked after her mother, hoping that care
and kindness would heal her too.

But Ella's mother got worse. Her father was
called home from his business trip.
And then the doctor told them
that Ella's mother wouldn't
ever get better.

Ella lay down on the bed,
wrapped her arms around
her mother, and cried.

Her mother stroked her
hair. "Precious girl," she said
softly. "Have courage, be
hopeful, and always be kind.
Promise me that, Ella,
whatever happens."

With tears in her eyes,
Ella promised.

2.

A YEAR LATER, as snow began to fall across the kingdom again, Ella's father remarried. His new wife and her two daughters came to live at the manor farm. Ella's father had barely been home since his wife had passed away, and Ella was excited that she would no longer be so alone.

"Just think, Tess, I have sisters now!" said Ella, scratching under the old dog's chin. "Grisella and Mona and I will do everything together—we will feed the animals and go for walks in the forest!"

But they didn't.

"Pigs!" snorted Grisella. "How disgusting—and so much work to move all that revolting mud!"

"Why would anyone want to walk in the woods?" asked Mona, looking stunned. "How exhausting!"

"We might find an injured rabbit," said Ella.

"Yuck! Dirty things!" said Grisella.

Be hopeful and kind, Ella thought, remembering the promise she'd made her mother. *Surely they'll change their minds once they meet my animal friends.*

But the sisters didn't change their minds. Ella and Tess went off to the woods by themselves, while Grisella and Mona slept late in their silk-covered beds. When they finally arose, they wouldn't make their beds. They didn't clean their rooms. Nor did they make their own breakfast.

At first, Ella did all of these things for them, but she didn't think it was very fair.

"Won't Grisella and Mona help me?" Ella asked her stepmother. "We will get everything done so much more quickly if we work together, and I'm sure my father—"

"Your father is away," snapped her stepmother. "I'm in charge, and you must do everything your sisters ask."

Be hopeful and kind, Ella thought to herself again as she cleaned and cooked without complaint. *And I will talk to my father when he returns.*

But he didn't. That very same winter, Ella's father was lost at sea when the ship he was sailing on was wrecked.

Ella was desolate. "Oh, Tess!" she sobbed. "What will happen to me now?" Tess licked her cheek.

Perhaps my sisters and I can comfort each other, she thought. Instead, soon after, Ella's stepmother announced that Ella would now eat in the kitchen. Alone.

"But why?" asked Ella.

"Your father is dead," her stepmother replied flatly, "and I can't bear the sight of you." *She must be so sad*, Ella realized. *I must remind her of my father.* And so she obeyed her stepmother and ate her meals in the kitchen with Tess.

Within the week, her stepmother told Ella to move out of her bedroom, so that Grisella and Mona could use it as a walk-in wardrobe. "You can sleep in the kitchen," she said coldly. "There's plenty of space by the fireplace." And, again, Ella obeyed her stepmother. But Ella was heartbroken, and that night, her tears spilled into the soot and ashes of the kitchen hearth as she huddled close to the fire, cuddling into Tess until she finally fell asleep.

The next morning, Ella awoke to see a very grumpy Grisella and Mona standing over her.

"Didn't you hear us ringing for our breakfast tea?" asked Grisella sharply.

"And look at you—there are cinders and soot all over you!" said Mona.

"Ha, cinders . . . Cinderella!" scoffed Grisella. "That's what we will call you now!"

"But it's not my name."

"Quiet, Cinderella!" ordered Mona. "And do hurry up with our tea."

And so Ella became Cinderella to her stepmother and sisters. Treated like a servant, she stayed down in the kitchen

and was allowed upstairs only when cleaning or serving. With no other family to turn to, and no money of her own, Ella had no choice but to stay. She did, however, have a choice in what she did when she was not cooking and cleaning, and so, early in the morning as the sun rose, Ella and Tess still went for long walks in the woods.

Slowly, the kitchen filled with the injured animals Ella brought home to nurse back to health. Three baby rabbits and a squirrel nestled close to the fire. Nightingales and cuckoos rested their bandaged wings in wicker baskets hung from the ceiling. There was even a family of six baby mice, who, having lost their mother, now huddled together in a teapot.

Caring for the animals always reminded Ella of her mother. She would not want her to be disheartened. "My name is Ella," she would declare, looking out the kitchen window at the star-filled night sky. "Take courage, be hopeful," she would say, talking to no one but herself—or so she thought.

3.

ONE SPRING DAY, as the trees began to blossom, there was a great commotion in the village square: the palace had decreed a royal ball. The king was getting old and wanted his son, the prince, married. So, as tradition dictated, he was inviting every lady in the land to a ball so the prince might choose his princess and the future queen.

"A royal ball, Tess," said Ella. The sheepdog was sitting by her feet in the kitchen as she prepared the morning's bread. "I would love to see the palace stables. They say the prince has many magnificent horses."

Ella's stepsisters had also heard the news and were quite deranged with excitement. They insisted on new dresses, new hairstyles, new shoes, and new jewels. Each was certain that the prince would choose her.

"I just know it will be me! Who could resist my beauty?" exclaimed Mona. "I must have a new dress that will match my gorgeous hair."

"Oh, dear sister," cried Grisella, not very dearly at all, "I really believe that it will be me whom the prince chooses! I must also have a new dress, one that highlights my divine green eyes."

"Cinderella!" both sisters screamed at once. "Cinderella, call for the dressmaker immediately!"

"But you have so many lovely dresses already," said Ella. "We could try some on!" *At last*, she thought, *something we can do all together.* "I thought I might wear one of my mother's dresses. It is—"

"It is not important," said her stepmother, entering the room. "You will not be going."

"But, Stepmother," began Ella, "all the ladies in the kingdom—"

"Exactly, girl," snapped her stepmother. "Ladies, not maids. A royal ball is no place for a servant."

So, on the night of the ball, Ella attended to her stepsisters. She painted their nails and threaded glittering beads through their hair. The stepsisters and their mother left for the ball without a word of thanks to Ella, who sat by the kitchen fire with tears in her eyes, hugging her mother's blue ball gown close to her heart. She looked out the open window at the night sky.

"Oh, why is their meanness rewarded?" she cried. "Mother told me always to be kind, but look where it's got me!" "I think your mother also told you to have courage, didn't she?" said a voice from outside.

In fright, Ella jumped up, dropping her mother's gown into the ashes of the hearth. "Who's out there," she asked in a shaky voice, "and how do you know about my mother?"

"Oh, we old people know things," said a little bent-over woman, smiling as she stepped inside. "Now, Ella, might I trouble you for a seat, and perhaps even a bowl of something? I'm a little tired and peckish."

"Of course!" said Ella. "Please forgive my rudeness. Come in and take my seat here by the fire. I'll warm you some soup."

The old woman sat by the fire and sipped her soup. By the glow of the fire Ella could see how gently the old woman looked at her.

"I feel much better now. Thank you, Ella."

"How do you know my name?" asked Ella.

"I am your fairy godmother," the woman said simply. "And I'm here to help. Now, where did I put my wand? We need to get you to that ball."

The woman pointed her long, silver wand at the ash-covered dress on the floor, and a bright light filled the room. Ella felt a rush of air, and the ashes from the hearth swirled up all around her, turning into glittering, sparkling, diamond-like flakes. When the light dulled, Ella looked down to see she was wearing her mother's gown, fully restored, and now with tiny woodland animals embroidered in silver thread around the hem and sash. On her feet were the most exquisite glass slippers.

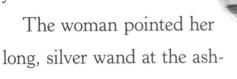

"My goodness!" exclaimed Ella. "Look at the stitching!"

Her fairy godmother smiled. Then she eyed a large pumpkin on the kitchen bench.

"That will do nicely," she declared. "Dear, please bring that outside for me. And that teapot of mice too, please."

Ella did as she was asked, placing the pumpkin and teapot on the ground in the farmyard. Her fairy godmother pointed her wand, and there was another flash of light. Then the most magnificent golden carriage appeared in front of Ella, sparkling with yet more diamonds and harnessed to six white horses, each with slightly longer tails than horses usually have.

"My goodness!" was all Ella could say again.

"Now we need a driver," said the fairy godmother, looking appraisingly at Tess. "And we need attendants, I think. Ah, yes, you two geese will be perfect."

With another wave of the wand and a flash, Tess was transformed into a carriage driver, and the two geese, Gabriel and Grace, became attendants, who bowed low to Ella as they held the carriage door open for her. "Madam," said Gabriel, smiling up at Ella, "your carriage awaits."

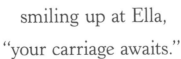

"Thank you, Gabriel," replied Ella, grinning as she stepped into the carriage. She turned to her fairy godmother. "How can I ever thank you?" she exclaimed.

"Kindness is its own reward," replied her fairy godmother. "Follow your good heart, Ella, and enjoy the ball—but make sure you leave by the last chime of midnight. Now, away!"

Tess shook the reins, and the six white horses began to trot. Then they broke into a canter, pulling the golden carriage through the manor-farm gates and off to the palace ball.

4.

WHEN ELLA ARRIVED at the palace, slightly late, all eyes turned toward her. Especially those of the prince. When Ella descended the stairs to the ballroom, he walked straight over to her and bowed.

"Madam, may I have the pleasure of this dance?" he asked.

"Yes, I'd like that," said Ella.

Ella and the prince danced, circling and twirling around and around the ballroom. When the dance ended, Ella was a little sorry.

"Shall we dance the next one as well?" asked the prince.

"Why not?" said Ella.

And so they did—and the next one, and the next.

"Who does she think she is?" Ella heard Grisella hiss to Mona as she swirled past them. She was relieved to discover that they did not recognize her. "And what a drab dress!"

"Selfish girl," Mona agreed snappily. "Keeping him to herself!"

But the prince only had eyes for Ella, and Ella liked the look of the prince, too. She particularly liked the way he pulled at his princely collar in between dances. "These frilly collars are a bit itchy," he confided when he saw her watching him.

"I know what you mean," said Ella. "These heels hurt a bit too."

"Shall we go outside for a while?" asked the prince.

"Yes, please," said Ella.

The prince took Ella out to the palace terrace. He unbuttoned his top two shirt buttons, and Ella took off her shoes.

"Ah, that's better!" they both said, which then made them both laugh.

"I don't really like all the palace pomp and ceremony," confided the prince. "This princess-finding ball is my father's idea. It's how we've always done things. I don't want to disobey him, but I think it might be time to look at things differently, do something new."

That made a lot of sense to Ella. She liked the way the prince thought.

"Look over there," said the prince, "beyond the palace gardens. That's where my horses are. That's where I'd like to be."

"I love horses too," said Ella, smiling. "Well, all animals, actually."

"I love riding in the woods," said the prince.

"I love the woods too!" cried Ella, smiling more. "I walk there every day with my dog, Tess."

"I have dogs too," said the prince. Ella's smile grew even wider. "I hunt deer with them."

Ella stopped smiling and started to frown. "Hunting is cruel," she said. "Why don't you protect the deer instead?"

"Well," began the prince, "we've always hunted. . . ."

"Mightn't it be time to look at things differently?" asked Ella, looking the prince straight in the eye. "Shouldn't we be kind to all living things?"

"Well," said the prince, "I hadn't—"

"I think it's important to be kind," said Ella. "Someone very important told me that."

"I think maybe you are right," said the prince, rather taken with this girl who wasn't afraid to speak her mind. "Would you like to see the horses?"

"I'd . . ."

But just then, the palace clock began to chime for midnight.

Dong! Dong!

"Oh, my goodness," cried Ella, "I need to go!"

"You do? Now? But why?"

Dong!

The chimes kept chiming. Ella wasn't sure what to say.

"I'm so sorry, I just do. Goodbye. I hope you find someone nice, I really do— and remember, no more hunting!"

"Don't go! Please!" cried the prince, but Ella had already scooped up her shoes and put them on as she fled down the palace steps. In her haste, she dropped one shoe. There was no time to stop to pick it up.

She reached the bottom of the stairs and leaped into the carriage. Tess, ever faithful, was waiting for her. "Quickly, Tess," Ella pleaded, "let's go. We don't have much time."

The carriage sped through the palace gates and down the road into the woods, toward the manor farm.

They were at a crossroads in the woods, still a ways from home, when the final chime sounded. The carriage slowed down. Then it stopped. *POP!* Ella was sitting in the dirt in her old dress, next to a pumpkin and six mice, with Gabriel and Grace pecking in the dirt, and Tess licking her hand. The one thing that remained was the glass slipper.

"I guess we'll have to walk home," said Ella, and sighed, eyeing the road leading to the manor farm. "Or, maybe . . ."

Ella looked at the glass slipper. It must be very valuable. She remembered what her mother had said: *Take courage.*

She remembered what her fairy godmother had said: *Follow your heart.*

And she remembered what the prince had said: *Do something new.*

Ella looked at Tess, her mice, and her geese, and she smiled. She picked up the glass slipper, and with her animals following her, she started walking down the other road, away from the manor farm. By morning, she would be far, far away.

84

5.

THE NEWS SPREAD across the kingdom: the prince was determined to find the girl who had so enchanted him with her passion and kindness—the owner of the dropped glass slipper. He and his courtier would travel the kingdom until the owner was found. Girls everywhere were desperate to try it on, for if it fit them, then they would become queen.

None were more desperate than Ella's two stepsisters. When the prince and his courtier arrived at the manor farm a few weeks later, they fell over each other to try on the shoe.

"It is my shoe, I'm telling you," cried Grisella, stuffing her foot into the much-too-small shoe.

"Don't listen to her," cried Mona, shoving her sister to the floor. "My foot will fit." But it didn't, of course— the slipper was much too big.

The prince's courtier checked his list. "How about Ella?" he inquired.

"Cinderella, you mean!" said Mona. "We haven't seen her since the night of the ball. She took off, stole two geese. Only has time for dirty animals, that one."

The prince, who had been waiting in the hallway, came into the room. "Did you say animals, madam?" he asked. "Yes, animals—she spends all her time with them," said Grisella. "Good riddance, if you ask me . . . Your Highness?"

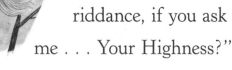

For the prince, on hearing that, had walked right out of the manor house, jumped on his horse with the glass slipper in his pocket, and ridden away.

One day a few weeks later, Ella was bringing some hay for the sheep into the stables of Kindness Farm. With the money from selling the precious glass slipper, Ella had bought a farm, and she was busy making it into a refuge for hurt animals.

"Hello," said a voice that she thought she recognized. "Could you use another pair of hands?"

Ella smiled when she turned around. It was the prince. He'd knelt down in front of Tess, who was licking his hand.

"Hello!" she replied. "That would be wonderful, thank you."

"And I'm pretty sure you have the other one of these?" said the prince, passing her the glass slipper.

"Well . . . I did," confessed Ella, taking off her rubber boot and slipping her foot into the slipper, which, of course, fit perfectly, "but I sold it to buy this animal sanctuary."

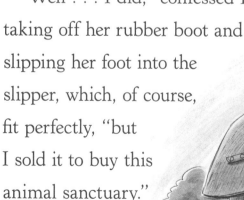

"Of course you did," said the prince. "Then perhaps you could take this?" He took a sack from his saddle and gently pulled out a rabbit. "I found it in a trap."

"You haven't been hunting?" asked Ella, squinting at the prince.

"Only for one thing," said the prince.

"What's that?" asked Ella, frowning.

"You," said the prince.

Ella took the rabbit and gave the prince a big hug. "If you're serious, there's a whole stable to clean out," she said.

"On it," said the prince, rolling up the sleeves of his very non-frilly, non-itchy shirt.

And Ella and the prince and all of the animals lived happily ever after at Kindness Farm.

Thumbelina

1.

ONCE upon a time a young woman lived in a cottage with a flower-filled garden, on the edge of a sweeping meadow and fields that burst with harvest.

The woman tended her garden lovingly, watching with joy each year as the first daffodils and violets appeared, followed

by perfumed jasmine, and then wisteria that draped the garden like a purple cloak.

Her vegetable garden filled with strawberries, snow peas, and cucumbers, and butterflies hovered in the lavender.

Every evening, from her spot on a white bench under a silver birch tree, the woman listened to the birds sing their last song and watched the sun sink. She was happy caring for her garden, but in a little corner of her heart she was lonely.

One day, an old woman in raggedy clothing came to the cottage gate asking for food. The young woman welcomed the stranger. She sat her down on the white bench in the shade, and brought her a pot of soothing chrysanthemum tea and a bowl of deliciously sweet berries, all from the garden.

The old woman was grateful. As she took her leave, she pulled a single large seed from her coat pocket. "Here, kind

woman," she said. "Take this, with my thanks. Plant it, and you will be blessed with your heart's longing."

The young woman planted the seed in a large stone pot. She thought no more of it until the next morning, when she was surprised to see that a long, single orange tulip had shot up in the pot overnight.

The petals of the flower were tightly shut, but as the woman sprinkled water over them, they slowly uncurled. The woman stood back in wonder when she saw a tiny girl lying at the flower's center, smiling up at her.

Tears of joy streaked the young woman's cheeks. "At last, a companion!" She lifted the tiny girl up on the palm of her hand. "You're so small—not even as tall as my thumb. I will call you Thumbelina, and we will be so happy in the garden together." And they were. The young woman and the tiny girl shared many wonderful times in the garden. Thumbelina was always inventing new games to play, and she loved to laugh and tell jokes.

Her laughter, almost like a song, would ring out over the garden and meadow, lifting the hearts of all who heard it. The young woman had placed a large dish on the garden table and filled it with water. When she was busy planting and weeding, Thumbelina would row up and down this dish on nasturtium-leaf boats, using horsehairs for oars, imagining she was the captain of a large boat sailing to unknown lands. She enlisted a family of ladybugs as her crew, and they would sail the water for hours, navigating their way through islands of fallen leaves.

"What is a bug's favorite sport?" Thumbelina called down from atop the nasturtium-stem mast.

The ladybugs shook their antennas.

"Cricket!" cried Thumbelina with a gleeful snort. "Now, my mates, to the end of the dish!"

Thumbelina would also help the neighborhood ants collect their food, carrying heavy seeds for them to their storehouse at the base of a large oak tree.

She would tell stories and jokes to the snails, encouraging them as they edged their way down the garden path, leaving glittering silver trails behind them.

"What do you call a snail on a ship? A snailor!"

Thumbelina loved playing with all her friends, but sometimes, peering out over the distant garden gate from her vantage point high up the ship's mast, she did wonder what it might be like to explore the vast meadow and fields that stretched as far as the eye could see, out in the world beyond the cottage. At night, lying in her polished-walnut-shell bed, with its violet-petal-padded mattress and rose petals for blankets, Thumbelina would often dream of the adventures she might have, the new friends she might meet in the meadow.

One morning, Thumbelina was helping the baby ladybugs with their flying practice. She longed to fly herself, and had woven some grass blades together to make little wings, but no one's attempts were very successful. The little beetles' wings popped out, fluttered furiously, and then fell back in under their shells, and Thumbelina's grass blades just caught a little gust of air, then sank. They all tumbled onto the soft grass in peals of beetle laughter. Thumbelina's laugh was the loudest of all, and it rang out over the cottage garden and gate, carrying as far away as the large lily-pad-filled pond on the other side of the meadow.

Which was where a large mother frog heard it.

"How beautiful," croaked the mother frog. "Such a happy sound! Whoever has that laugh would make a fine plaything for my froglings."

And with that, the mother frog leaped across the meadow, over the garden gate, and onto Thumbelina's table. She picked up a surprised Thumbelina in her big mouth and took her back to her lily-pad pond.

"This is your home now," croaked the mother frog imperiously. She placed Thumbelina on a raft of joined-up lily pads by the side of the pond, next to her eight froglings, who were about Thumbelina's size and who hopped over each other in delighted shock upon seeing her—for they had never seen a tiny girl such as Thumbelina before.

Now, Thumbelina had quite enjoyed the ride, and the little frogs did look rather fun, but she didn't want to live on the pond. "Please take me home," she said firmly.

The mother frog shook her head. "You must stay here, with my froglings."

"Listen here," began Thumbelina indignantly, "you can't treat me like a plaything just because I'm little."

"That's exactly why I want you," croaked the mother frog, a

little impatiently. "You're different. I haven't seen a tiny child like you for such a long time."

"What?" shouted Thumbelina, astounded. "A child like me? What do you mean?"

"You know: tiny girl, lovely laugh," said the mother frog. "Now, I see you're going to be difficult."

And with that, she picked Thumbelina up in her mouth again and, in one giant leap, hopped onto a single lily pad sitting all alone in the middle of the pond and set Thumbelina upon it. She croaked delightedly as she hopped away.

But Thumbelina wasn't delighted. She sat back on the lily pad and thought about how to escape.

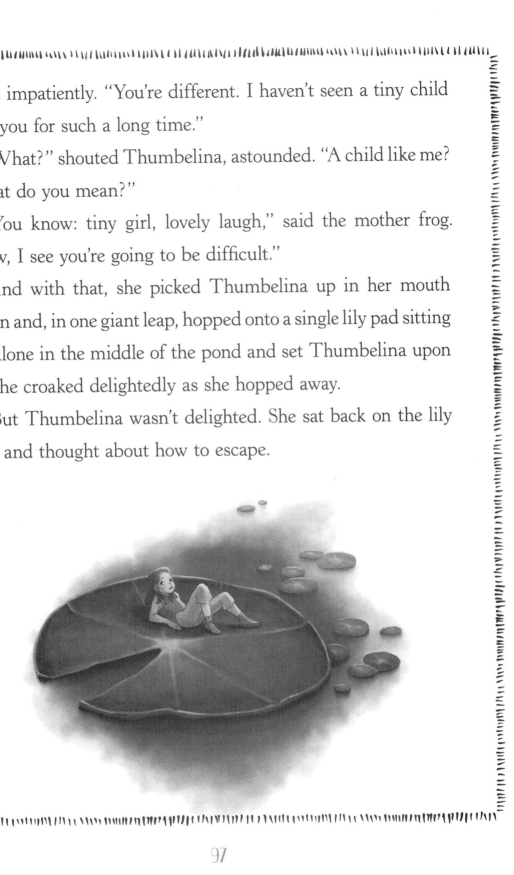

2.

THUMBELINA LOOKED DOWN into the pond and saw three minnows swimming past the lily leaf. She watched them nibble at its stem underwater—and that gave her an idea.

"Hello there!" she cried. The minnows popped their heads above the water, their eyes bulging inquisitively. "Might I trouble you for some help? Would you mind nibbling all the way through this lily-pad stem?"

The minnows turned to look at each other. The lily-pad stem was delicious, after all. And so they nibbled away until, just as Thumbelina had hoped, the lily pad was set free of its stem and began to float away.

Thumbelina had hoped the lily pad would float all the way to the side of the pond, but the current was weak, and she simply floated around in circles. *This is no use*, she thought, looking up at the sky just as a white butterfly settled on a water reed above her. Another idea struck Thumbelina.

"Hello!" she shouted to the butterfly. "Might you come over here? Oh, and please bring that reed with you."

The butterfly looked a little surprised,
but obediently clutched a long, thin reed
with its front legs and fluttered over.
As it hovered over Thumbelina,
she grabbed the reed. "Now to
the bank, please, if you will," she
cried. "Would you like to hear
a joke while we are floating?"

The butterfly tilted its
antennae down toward Thumbelina.

"Why wouldn't they let the butterfly into the dance?"
asked Thumbelina. "Because . . . it was a mothball!"

"Good one," said the butterfly, wings fluttering in
amusement. And, just a few jokes later,
Thumbelina and the butterfly had
reached the edge of the pond.

"Thank you!" said Thumbelina.
"If I can ever return the
favor, do let me know!"

The butterfly fluttered
away, still chuckling.

Hands on hips, Thumbelina

looked up and all around her. It was late summer. Above her, long stalks of wild grass waved and glistened in the sunshine. Cicadas chirped, and wildflowers dotted the vast landscape. "The meadow," she exclaimed. "I'm here!"

Thumbelina remembered what the mother frog had said about there being other tiny children like her. Perhaps they were hidden somewhere in this very meadow. Right then and there, she decided that she wouldn't go home, but would stay and search for them instead.

Thumbelina was excited, and perhaps a little nervous, but before she had taken even one single tiny nervous or excited step, a beetle swooped down over her head and snatched her up in its feet.

"Hey!" yelled Thumbelina.

The beetle flew higher and higher, carrying Thumbelina up to the top of a large oak tree before setting her down on a branch, alongside a whole group of other beetles. The view was magnificent.

"Hey!" Thumbelina yelled again, trying to uncurl the beetle's legs from around her waist. "What's going on?"

"I've never seen a tiny girl like you before," said the beetle. "My friends will think you are very interesting."

Thumbelina sighed. And then she stopped struggling, and

tried to look as uninteresting as she could. *No jokes for them,* she thought.

"Look what I've brought!" buzzed the beetle to his friends.

But Thumbelina's plan seemed to work—the other beetles weren't at all interested in her.

"No shell," buzzed one.

"No wings," buzzed another.

"No antennae," chirped in a third.

"Odd," judged another. "Not one of us."

Thumbelina hadn't wanted to be with the beetles, but she couldn't help but feel a little hurt by the rejection. The beetle who'd caught her looked disappointed too. When Thumbelina asked it to take her back to the ground, it complied, dropping her at the base of the tree.

"That's better!" said Thumbelina. "Now, where was I? Ah, yes, searching. I'd never imagined there'd be other tiny children like me. I wonder what it would be like to meet some. . . ."

So Thumbelina set out to see.

3.

THE DAYS TURNED into weeks as Thumbelina made her way across the meadow. She found plenty to eat, munching contentedly on pollen sandwiches, and on blueberries that she cut into segments using a knife she made from bark. She sipped on dew from leaves, and used daisies as sun umbrellas.

She met many new friends on her way across the meadow—caterpillars, ladybugs, grasshoppers—and she asked them all if they had seen any other little children like her. Sadly, no one had, but Thumbelina was determined and kept walking.

"Hello," she said one day to a mother rabbit and her fourteen baby rabbits. "Have you ever met a little girl like me around the meadow?"

"I don't think I have," replied the mother rabbit distractedly, counting off her children as they hopped down into their burrow.

Thumbelina thought the mother rabbit looked a little

harried, what with all those children to look after. *Perhaps a joke will cheer her up*, she thought. "One more thing: What do you call a happy rabbit?"

"A happy rabbit? No idea, I'm sure," replied the mother rabbit.

"A hoptimist!" cried Thumbelina.

The fourteenth bunny, who was about to hop into the hole, fell backward laughing at the joke, but the mother rabbit simply twitched her nose.

"Oh, yes, I see," she said, picking the last baby bunny up by the scruff of its neck with her teeth and scurrying toward the hole. "Can't stop longer, sorry—family calls."

Thumbelina felt a bit glum after that. *Does my family call?* she wondered. She took a deep breath. "Onward!" she told herself aloud. And so she pressed on across the meadow.

Another day, after summer had turned into autumn, Thumbelina heard a swarm of bees above her. "Hello!" she called up to them as they landed on one of the season's last sunflowers. "Have you seen any little children as you've flown around? Perhaps in a flower?"

"No," buzzed the bees.

"Oh," said Thumbelina, a little dejected—until another joke came to her. "What kind of bee can't make up its mind?"

"Hmmm, don't know," buzzed one of the bees.

"A maybe!" shouted Thumbelina.

"Oh, that's rather good!" they all buzzed, heading off. "We must tell the queen. Good luck finding your friends!"

Thumbelina kept traveling and meeting other insects and animals of the meadow, and they all wished her well too . . . but none had seen any little children like her. As the weeks turned into months, Thumbelina couldn't help starting to feel more than a little bit sad.

Surely I can't be the only little child in the whole world, she thought one day, as she climbed up a dandelion stalk to get a better view. A flock of swallows flew past. She hadn't met any swallows yet on her journey. "Hello!" she shouted. "Excuse me!"

But the swallows didn't stop, and Thumbelina grew sadder. She didn't think to wonder why the swallows seemed so determined to leave the meadow; nor did she notice that the air was turning chilly and the leaves were starting to fall from the trees. But she *did* notice when the rain came. Heavy drops of rain pelted down on her. The wind blew stronger, and it was hard climbing through all the fallen leaves.

When the snow began to fall, Thumbelina dodged the snowflakes as best she could. The snow coated the branches of the trees, and Thumbelina was both cold and afraid. Now all the animals seemed to have left the meadow, and she was alone.

"Brrr," she shivered one night, snuggling into a heap of fallen oak leaves. "What shall I do now? Perhaps a joke will cheer me up. Hmmm, I know—what did one firefly say to the other? You glow, girl! Ha!"

Thumbelina chuckled, and the chuckle became a laugh, and the laugh was swept up in the wind and blew its way to a field mouse who was gathering the last acorns from under another oak tree for its winter store. The laugh made the little mouse twitch its nose, and it walked toward the sound to find Thumbelina shivering in the withered oak leaves.

"What a lovely laugh you have," said the mouse. "But, my goodness, you're freezing! Come with me and I'll make you a cup of dandelion tea." And it took Thumbelina to its little cottage made of mud and twigs on the side of a mound.

It was cozy and warm inside, and the mouse's pantry was stocked with delicious berries and nuts it had gathered during summer.

The field mouse made Thumbelina a lovely cup of dandelion tea, in an acorn cupule. "Oh, thank you," said Thumbelina, who was wrapped up in a quilt stuffed with dried petals. "I feel so much better now."

The field mouse loved Thumbelina's laugh and thought it would be helpful to have an extra pair of paws around the house over the winter. The mouse had many family members coming to stay, and it was hard to keep things tidy.

Thumbelina gratefully agreed to stay. All winter, she swept the cottage floor with a thistle broom, prepared meals, and told jokes to the many mice that came to visit. It was jolly, but Thumbelina sometimes felt a twinge of secret sadness.

They are all so happy, these mice, being mice together. Will I ever find the other tiny children? Wherever could they be hiding?

One day Thumbelina had stepped outside the cottage into the snow to empty the walnut trash shells when she saw a swallow lying on the ground, panting for breath.

"Oh my," cried Thumbelina. "What's happened to you?"

The swallow could hardly talk. Thumbelina leaned in close. "I couldn't keep up with the other birds flying to warmer lands," it whispered. "The winds were too much for me, and I had to land. Now I fear I will never rejoin my family."

"Don't worry," Thumbelina said, stroking its wing. "I will help you become strong again."

The swallow was much too large for the mouse's cottage, so Thumbelina, using all her strength, pushed it into the hollow of a nearby tree. And every day after that, when she left the cottage to empty the walnut shells, she would visit the swallow, feeding and encouraging it. (The swallow's favorite joke was: What do you give a bird who is not feeling well? Tweetment!) As the snow began to melt in the meadow, the swallow regained its strength and its spirit.

4.

ONE DAY THUMBELINA noticed that
the air no longer had a chill to it. She saw
that the snow had all melted away, and
that tiny flowers were beginning to
appear—snowdrops and blue-and-
white hyacinths, pushing through
the cold ground.

"Look," Thumbelina said to
the swallow. "Spring is coming!"

"And look at me," chirped
the swallow, flapping its wings
and hovering in the air. "I am flying! I am well again! I'm
ready to find my family," said the swallow. "Come with me!
You might find your family too."

Thumbelina shook with excitement. "Yes, let's go!" She
dashed inside to hug the surprised field mouse goodbye, and
then she climbed onto the swallow's back. The swallow took
off and they soared up into the sky.

Thumbelina could scarcely believe her eyes. They flew over the meadow she'd spent so many months exploring in just seconds, then over another meadow, and another . . . then some woods, and even an ocean, until at last, days later, they reached another land. As the swallow began to descend, Thumbelina could see that it was a land full of flowers.

"My flower!" she shouted. "They are all like the flower I was born in—and look, there are so many, and so many different colors: blue ones, pink ones, purple ones!"

The swallow swooped lower still, then landed on a tuft of grass in the middle of a flower field. Thumbelina climbed off the swallow's back. The moment she stepped onto the ground, she felt strangely at home.

"Hello!" she bellowed. "Is there anyone here?"

Somehow, Thumbelina just knew that there would be—and, sure enough, little girls and boys started to emerge from behind the stalks of the flowers. Tiny girls and boys just like Thumbelina.

"Hello," said a little girl, stepping out from a yellow flower.

And, "Hello," said a boy from a red flower. "I love your wings."

"My what?" said Thumbelina.

"Your wings," repeated the boy.

"But I don't have . . . ," began Thumbelina, as she reached behind her and felt between her shoulder blades. "Oh my goodness, I do have wings! *Look, swallow!*"

"Yes, Thumbelina," said the swallow. "We can fly on adventures together."

"Oh yes, let's," said Thumbelina. "I will show you my garden and my friends there."

"I can't wait," said the swallow. "But now that you have found your family, it is time for me to get back to mine." And with that, the swallow flapped its wings and swooped up into the sky.

My family, realized Thumbelina as she waved farewell to the swallow. *Yes, this is my family!*

Thumbelina laughed, and it was with such joy that, to her surprise, it caused her wings to flutter. This made her laugh even more, which made her wings flutter even more. . . . The other children started laughing too, and their wings began to flutter, and they all rose up into the sky. Thumbelina was flying!

"Hey," said Thumbelina, flying up to one boy, "do you know why fairies don't live under toadstools?"

"No," said the boy. "Why?"

"Because . . . there's not mushroom!" cried Thumbelina delightedly, rising even higher into the sky.

The boy laughed. The other children laughed too, and Thumbelina beamed. A chorus of laughter echoed throughout the flower field as the flower boys and girls flew higher and higher into the sky.

And they all lived happily ever after.